Text copyright © 1989 by Eric Houghton. Illustrations copyright © 1989 by Denise Teasdale.
First American Edition 1990 published by Orchard Books. First published in Great Britain by Aurum Books for Children.
All rights reserved. No part of this book may be reproduced or transmitted in any form or by any means, electronic or
mechanical, including photocopying, recording or by any information storage or retrieval system, without permission
in writing from the Publisher. Orchard Books, 387 Park Avenue South, New York,
NY 10016.Manufactured in the United States of America. Printed by General Offset Co., Inc. Bound by Horowitz / Rae.
Book design by Mina Greenstein. The text of this book is set in 14 pt. Meridien.
The illustrations are pen and ink and watercolors, reproduced in four colors.   10   9   8   7   6   5   4   3   2

Library of Congress Cataloging-in-Publication Data

Houghton, Eric. Walter's magic wand: story / by Eric Houghton; illustrations by Denise Teasdale. — 1st American ed.
p.   cm.   "First published in Great Britain by Aurum Books for Children" — T.p. verso. Summary: Feeling restless at the
library, Walter combines his imagination with his magic wand to bring several exotic books to life and complicate the
librarian's tidy existence. ISBN 0–531–05851–4. ISBN 0–531–08451–5 (lib. bdg.)   [1. Libraries — Fiction.   2. Books
and reading — Fiction.   3. Imagination — Fiction.]   I. Teasdale, Denise, ill.   II. Title. PZ7.H8144Wal   1989
[E] — dc20   89–35400 CIP AC

Walter's Magic Wand

BY **Eric Houghton**

ILLUSTRATED BY **Denise Teasdale**

ORCHARD BOOKS   NEW YORK

Walter made a magic wand from a stick he found in his backyard. He covered it with scraps of colored paper and waved it around.

"Does it work?" asked his mother.
"Only when I say the magic words," he said.

That afternoon his mother took him to the library. Walter brought his magic wand with him.

"Please don't poke," said the librarian, when Walter pushed some papers off her desk.

"Please don't meddle," said the librarian, when Walter played with the index cards.

"Please don't touch," said the librarian, when he built a castle with her biggest dictionaries. Walter stared at her.

"Walter, find a book to read— and stay out of trouble," said his mother.

Walter went over to a bookcase. He gave
a practice wave with his magic wand.
"Ploppa-gooksniff," he said, saying the first
magic words that came into his head. Then he
tapped a book called *Tigers*.

Trees and bushes sprouted from the floor. Vines and orchids twisted around the bookshelves. Apes swung from the overhead lights, and snakes slithered along the magazine racks.

Walter felt hot and sticky.

Seven tigers appeared from behind the bookcases. They were snarling and looked very hungry.

Walter was delighted.

But the librarian did not get eaten. She helped everyone climb to the top of the tallest bookcase. Then she sprinkled thumbtacks on the floor. The tigers tried to reach her, but they couldn't.

"And please don't scratch the furniture with those claws," the librarian told them.

Walter was disappointed. He thought the tigers should have been braver. He reached down with his magic wand and tapped the book called *Tigers*.

At once the jungle disappeared.
   "Haven't you found a book yet, Walter?"
asked his mother.

Walter could see the librarian standing at her desk watching him. He went over to another bookcase.

"Oogla-pluntium," he said. He tapped another book with his magic wand. It was called *Pirates*.

Sand covered the floor. Palm trees and rocks grew out of it. Parrots flew around the bookshelves and lizards scuttled over the encyclopedias.

Walter felt dry and dusty.

Eleven pirates leaped out from behind a
bookcase looking for someone to kidnap.
Walter was pleased at how fierce they looked.

But the librarian was not dragged off in chains. Piling up her fattest dictionaries, she built a fortress on her desk and gathered everyone inside. When the pirates waved their swords and shouted bloodcurdling threats, the librarian shot pencils at them with a rubber band and drove them away.

"And please don't damage the books with those swords," she told them.

Walter was disappointed. He thought the pirates should have tried harder. He reached out with his magic wand and tapped the book called *Pirates*. At once the pirates disappeared.

"Don't stand around dreaming, Walter,"
said his mother. "Find a book!"

Walter could see the librarian behind her desk, frowning. He stepped over to another bookcase.

"Quoggley-squint-box," he said. He tapped another book with his magic wand. It was called *Oceans*.

Waves surged through the library. Seaweed climbed over the counters. Lobsters crawled among the books. Dolphins splashed and played.

Walter felt cold and wet.

But the librarian was not swept away. As the waves rose higher and higher, she quickly built a boat with three bookcases. They were labeled A, R, and K. Then she helped everyone on board and they sailed around the library, using atlases for paddles.

"And please stop balancing those picture books on your noses," she told the dolphins.

Walter forgot to be disappointed. He was too busy enjoying himself. His atlas made bigger splashes than anyone else's.

After a while he leaned out of the boat and tapped the book called *Oceans* with his magic wand. At once the ocean disappeared.

"Do you want all of those, Walter?" asked his mother. "I thought you were just daydreaming...."

Walter looked down. He was holding three books: one about tigers, one about pirates, and one about oceans.

He took them to the desk and watched the librarian stamp them. Then he threw his magic wand into the trash. He knew the magic couldn't really have happened.

"But that magic wand of yours is much too good to throw away!" said the librarian, and she took it out of the trash and put it back in his hand.

Walter stared at her.

It was then that he noticed the piece of palm leaf caught in her hair, the seaweed poking from her collar, and her sudden smile.